Bettendorf Public Library
Informa
www.betten ⊲ S0-BAI-748

WITHDRAWN

Twicetold Tales is published by Stone Arch Books
A Capstone Imprint
1710 Roe Crest Drive
North Mankato, Minnesota 56003
www.capstonepub.com

© 2014 Stone Arch Books

All rights reserved. No part of this publication may be
reproduced in whole or in part, or stored in a retrieval
system, or transmitted in any form or by any means,
electronic, mechanical, photocopying, recording, or
otherwise, without written permission of the publisher.

Library of Congress Cataloging-in-Publication Data
Snowe, Olivia.
  The girl and the seven thieves / by Olivia Snowe;
illustrated by Michelle Lamoreaux.
       p. cm. -- (Twicetold tales)
  Summary: In this modern version of Snow White, Eira
Blanc escapes when her stepmother tries to have her
killed, and finds herself taken in by seven thieves who
agree to help her in her plan to take down the Wicked
Witch of the West Side.
  ISBN 978-1-4342-6018-5 (library binding) -- ISBN
978-1-4342-6280-6 (paper over board)
1. Fairy tales. 2. Folklore--Germany. 3. Stepmothers-
-Folklore. 4. Witches--Folklore. [1. Fairy tales. 2.
Folklore. 3. Stepmothers--Folklore. 4. Witches--
Folklore.] I. Lamoreaux, Michelle, ill. II. Snow White
and the seven dwarfs. English. III. Title.

  PZ8.S41763Gir 2013
  398.20943--dc23

                         2013002780

Designer: Kay Fraser
Vector Images:: Shutterstock

Printed in the United States of America in
Stevens Point, Wisconsin.
032013   007227WZF13

The Girl and the Seven Thieves

by Olivia Snowe

illustrated by Michelle Lamoreaux

STONE ARCH BOOKS™

FIC
SNOW

You know the story.

You've heard it before.

Everyone has.

Now, read it again.

A new twist. A new gasp.

The story is told again.

TWICETOLD.

1

I've been sitting here for like an hour. My beautiful and insane stepmother told me to come. She sent Hunter, the old valet, to fetch me.

I'd just finished supper, and though I adore good old Hunter, I was trying to enjoy a little sunshine on the rooftop patio before heading out for an evening with my friends.

Our apartment is the top three floors of a

high-rise right on Central Park in Manhattan. It's not too shabby, as my dad likes to say.

"Lady Eira," Hunter said as he stepped onto the veranda. That's me. I mean, not the Lady part. He's just silly like that. I'm just Eira. It means "snow" in Welsh.

"Her Majesty"—he meant my stepmom, queen in her own mind—"requires the honor of your company in her personal study directly," Hunter said.

"Directly," I learned rather quickly after my dad married the "queen," means "right now." So I got up from my towel and chaise, pulled a sundress on over my bathing suit, and followed Hunter inside.

"Directly," I should explain, only applies to me. My stepmom can take her sweet time. I've had an hour to stare blankly around the queen's study.

Funny thing about the study: it's really my mom's studio. Or it was, until she died.

Then my dad remarried.

A New York minute after my dad said "I do," the queen paraded in here with an entourage of contractors, decorators, and curators. She tore out all my mom's photography supplies, took down all her photos, and remade the room as an office fit for a queen—albeit one with awful taste.

I was four then. I'm sixteen now.

I remember my real mom, but hardly at all. I remember her smile, which was as big a smile as you can imagine, and it gleamed white between ruby-red lips. Her skin was like ivory, and her hair like ebony, but in all other respects she was nothing like a piano.

She looked just like me, and I have pictures to prove it.

My stepmom looks like us, too: She's pale as death, though, not as ivory or snow or a lonely cloud. And her lips are red like fresh blood, not a ruby. And her hair is black like a haunted dungeon or the deep dark of a wolf's den, not like a summer midnight or wet ink.

We don't get along, my stepmother and I. This wouldn't be too big a deal—it's a large apartment—but most of the time, she's my only parental unit. Dad travels for business almost nonstop. I suppose apartments like this don't come cheap.

My friend Giselle claims the queen is jealous of the princess, like we're living in some old fairy tale and I'm too beautiful to have around. It's crazy.

Giselle also claims the queen is a witch— which is not as crazy as it sounds.

A couple of years ago, one of the staff spoke sharply to my stepmother. Apparently the staff person—it was Lucy, from the laundry service—hadn't done a perfect job removing a "pomegranate juice" stain from a white handkerchief.

It was on my stepmom's favorite hanky, too,

and I don't for a moment believe the stain was pomegranate juice, but that's not the point.

Stepmom summoned Lucy and scolded her. Lucy, though, didn't put up with it. After all, she'd washed clothes for my mother for years, and my mother never spoke to anyone unkindly.

"The stain won't come out," Lucy said. I imagine she set her jaw and clasped her hands. "I'm not a magician."

"Then you're fired," said the queen. She no doubt waved her away. "Out of my sight."

"How dare you!" Lucy said, and we're all very proud of her to do this day.

But the queen shook with rage, and she shouted, "Out of my sight or I'll snap your neck!" in her loudest, most terrifying voice. Lucy was brave, certainly, but not made of steel. She fled the office and fled the building. She never came back.

But the queen wasn't satisfied. For the next

twelve months, the workers in the laundry service—every last one of them—suffered grave injuries, weird diseases, and financial ruin.

When Abraham, the laundry staff chief, broke both his legs in a freak dryer accident—they say he'll never walk again—perhaps the queen was satisfied. That was the last of the laundry incidents.

Giselle—and most of the staff—claims it was witchcraft, and that Stepmother is the witch. I don't believe a word of it. I think my stepmom is a lot of things, but a witch?

2

I'm sitting in her office guest chair, looking
at a horrible sculpture, a painting that looks
like the work of a three-year-old, and a view of
Central Park through the grandest windows on
the west side. There's not a raven, spellbook, or
bubbling cauldron in sight.

"There you are, Eira," she says as she
appears in her office and strides across the
million-dollar rug, as if I might have been
someplace else and she'd been searching

absolutely everywhere. "I have an errand for you."

She sits at her desk and her face flashes— in an instant she is the picture of pleasant. Sometimes she seems so kind and beautiful and nice.

"You're well?" she asks, her smile as sincere as you please, the colors of her teeth and lips like bone and blood.

I shrug. "I'm fine."

"Grand," she says, and the moment is passed. Her smile is gone. "So. An errand. Hunter will escort you."

She is scribbling on a pad—she keeps these pads all over the house. They're square and seem made of pressed paper pulp and gold flecks, and they probably are. She tears the sheet from the pad and reaches across her desk—just a little, so I still have to get up and reach most of the way to grab the paper.

It's just got an address on it—not one I

recognize, way uptown. It might even be in the Bronx.

"What's the errand?" I ask, but the queen is already on her feet, which means—house rules—I have to stand too.

She ushers me out of the room. "Hunter will explain everything," says my stepmom. "Please do hurry. I want Hunter back as soon as possible."

"Okay," I say to the door as it closes in my face.

Hunter is standing there in the hall. "This way, Lady Eira, come on," he says, and he's smiling. But his voice sounds a bit off. Just something weird about it. I can't put my finger on what it is. I don't know.

I follow him toward the elevator. "Is everything all right, Hunter?" I ask.

He glances quickly over his shoulder at me and flashes another fake smile.

"Fine, fine," he says, as brightly as ever. "You know I always get nervous running important errands for Her Highness."

I pretend to chuckle, but Hunter's nerves are shakier than normal. Something's up.

~3~

On family outings with my dad and the queen, we keep to ourselves. We often put the opaque window up between us and the driver's seat, even. But when it's just me and Hunter, we like to keep things informal.

"So," I say, leaning forward in the back seat. "Where are we going?"

"Is your seatbelt on?" Hunter says. He's dodging the question.

I lean back and clip in. "It's cool," I say. "Secrets are cool."

But it's not cool for long. The limo slips onto the West Side Highway, and now we're zooming along Manhattan Island to its end at the Bronx.

"Seriously, Hunter," I say, calling over the roar of the traffic and the engine and sounds of the city. "Where are we going? Why am I on this errand?"

He doesn't even flinch, so maybe he can't hear me, but I'm beginning to get weirded out.

When he pulls off the highway and crawls through the streets of the Bronx—unfamiliar streets; crowded streets; dirty streets—I try the door handle.

Locked.

"Hunter!" I snap.

This time he flinches. "I'm sorry, Eira," he says, hardly loud enough to hear.

The limo slips from the wide main avenue and down a narrow side street.

Cars are double-parked. The locals congregate on stoops. They lean on the hoods of their old, rusting cars and their new, flamboyant SUVs. At least three different songs boom from apartment windows and car stereos.

"It's not much farther," Hunter says. After a beat, he adds, "You're going to be okay."

The limo lurches as he turns slowly off the street, up a bumpy driveway, and into an alley barely wide enough for the car.

"What is this?" I say. I finally stop tugging at the door handle. "Hunter, tell me what's going on."

But he doesn't answer. He just opens his door and climbs out of the car. A moment later, mine opens, and Hunter offers his hand. It's like instead of stopping in some smelly, desolate alley deep in the Bronx, we have just pulled up to the Waldorf for one of Dad's big charity dinners.

But I'm not wearing a gown, and Hunter's not wearing his driving suit. I'm in a sundress over my bathing suit.

I don't even have my handbag. I don't even have my phone.

"I'm not getting out," I say, and I slide across the huge seat and cross my arms.

"Please, Eira," Hunter says. "I have to be quick or her ladyship will begin to check on us."

"Then take me home," I say. "I'll explain everything to her."

Hunter leans in, with both his gloved hands on the seat. "It's impossible," he says, shaking his head.

"What is impossible, Hunter?" I ask.

"Eira," he says, his eyes red and tired, his voice rough and worn. "Dear. She wants me to kill you. She wants me to strangle you and leave you here in this alley."

My face goes cold and my whole body gets tingly and itchy. In an instant, my eyes are full of tears, and then Hunter's are too.

He crawls another foot into the backseat and reaches for me, so I swing my knees up, throw my back against the door, and kick up my foot, right into his nose.

He screams and pulls back his head, and it crashes into the roof of the car. The blood starts from his nose in a drip at first, and then flows freely.

Hunter sits back and cups his hands over his nose, swearing up a storm.

"I'm not going to kill you, Eira!" he shouts, as if to be heard over the flow of his blood and the sobbing from my chest.

"Then let me go now," I say, barely a whisper.

"I was going to," Hunter says, leaning his head back. He looks at me sideways over the tips of his bloody fingers. "The door's unlocked behind you."

I check, and it is. I shove it.

The door swings open and bangs into a garbage can.

"Careful," he says. "You'll scratch the paint."

So I slam it again, and then again, and then one more time. "Tell her she won't get away with this."

He shakes his head. "I'm going to tell her you're dead, beautiful," Hunter says. "Or I'll be dead."

I climb out backwards and look at Hunter a moment. Then I look up the alley toward the crowded side street—a foreign country. "What should I do?"

Hunter reaches one bloody hand into his

pants pocket and pulls out an envelope. He reaches it out to me. "It's not a lot," he says. "A few of us pitched in."

I open the envelope. It's stuffed with cash. There's a decent stack of it, sure, but not enough to stay alive in the Bronx all by myself for long.

"I can't," I say, reaching it out to him. "Besides, I can't walk around this neighborhood with that much cash. It's not safe. It'd be a liability."

"You're probably right," Hunter says, shaking his head with a big sigh. "Whatever, Eira. Just get out of here. Find a way out of town, even. Head to the trains. Go to Jersey or Upstate. Get lost."

He reaches across and gives me a little shove. Then he pulls the door closed. I hear the locks fall into place.

I can't see him through the black-tinted windows, but he must have climbed into the front seat, because a moment later the limo roars to life and the tires squeal as he pulls away, leaving me pressed against a garbage can with nowhere to go.

The action on the street has doubled with the setting of the sun. I do my best to pass unnoticed, but that isn't happening.

"Hey, beautiful," someone shouts from a stoop or an idling sports car.

"You lost, baby?" shouts someone else. I feel the crowd find me. I feel it swell. I feel them move toward me.

I put my head down and walk faster. I slip

between men and boys, and I hear the women call out. They say things like, "Leave her alone," and "What's she doing here?"

Then I run, and they laugh at me, but I don't care. I run until I reach the big avenue at the corner.

Then I turn and run some more, till the rain starts.

I duck into a bus shelter and almost smile when the inviting glow of a for-hire taxi appeared on the nearly empty avenue.

"Taxi!" I shout, throwing out my arm, waving it around.

The cab pulls up, and I have to jump back to avoid being splashed by its wake. I climb in quickly.

"Hi," I say, offering my biggest, brightest smile. The driver doesn't even notice. "So, I have to get to Central Park West, but I don't have any money."

Now he notices. He gives me the old withering glance in the rearview.

"But where I'm going, there's loads of money," I add quickly, "and someone will be able to pay you. And tip you really well."

"Out," he says. "Wait for the bus."

"I don't have money for the bus," I say.

"Exactly," the driver says. "Out."

I lean forward, so my forehead is right against the thick plastic divider between us. "Listen," I say, in my kindest and gentlest begging voice. "I really need help. I know it's a lot to take on faith, but I promise to make it worth your while. You can charge whatever you like."

He gives me a long look in the mirror, his mouth twisted in disbelief, and for an instant— for a wonderful, soul-quenching moment—I think I have him. But it's gone. He pulls away his gaze. "Out."

"You're a bad, bad man," I say, but I climb out, because I don't want to kick anyone else in the face if it comes to an altercation in the backseat. The cabbie speeds away, and this time I'm not quick enough to avoid the spray. The hem of my sundress—already smelling of back-alley trash cans—is now speckled with muddy water.

I wish I'd accepted Hunter's cash. All I can do now is find a stoop, someplace hidden and dry, and cry the night away. But when I look up from my disgusting and mangled dress, I see three figures—the only other people on the avenue—walking toward me.

Casually—because there's no reason to overreact, or make it look like I'm overreacting, anyway—I turn and walk slowly the other way. But immediately, I spot another three people coming from that way.

I'm stuck on this block. I can't run across the street. That would make me look like a victim right away. So I don't see how I can avoid these people.

I take a deep breath. They're not criminals. They're just people, probably walking home. And in the rain, too, just like me. If anything, they'll feel some empathy toward me, like I should for them.

There's an alcove in the middle of the block. I spot it and head there at once, my head down, my legs moving quickly over long strides.

The rain coats my face now, plastering my hair to my forehead and ears and the back of my neck, but I don't care. I can just make out the faces of the men coming toward me from the farther corner.

They're close, and they're smiling—not pleasantly.

I'm into the alcove, and the moment I'm out of sight, I start to run. It cuts clear through the block, sheltered above, like a pedestrian tunnel through the belly of a building. My feet ring on the giant marble tiles. It's slippery, but I can't slow down. Behind me, the men are running too.

I'm halfway through. The tunnel is lit with dim, square fixtures above me, a gross yellow color. The rhythm of my feet as I run matches the rhythm of the light flashing in my eyes.

At the far end, one light is out, and the last light flickers and cracks randomly. One instant the far end is pitch dark, and the next it flashes brightly, like lightning cracking across the sky at night.

I'm only paces away when the light flashes out and the alcove goes dark. Behind me, all six men are following. I glance over my shoulder, and there they are.

But they're not hurrying. I'm nearly through the alcove, and they're not hurrying. As I turn my head again and the light flashes on, I know why.

A seventh figure waits for me at the alcove's exit.

I skid to a stop, my hands up—fingers splayed, nails out, ready to claw—but he just grabs my wrists and says, "Boo."

"Let me go!" I snap at him, kicking at his legs as he dodges and laughs.

"Easy, girl," he says through his snickers, like I'm an agitated horse or something. The rest of the gang comes up behind me, but they don't touch me. Finally the seventh lets go of my wrist and I slap his face.

He makes an "ooh" face and rubs his cheek. "Wow," he says. "That was uncalled for."

He must be crazy. Uncalled for? I'm surrounded by seven men!

Okay, a couple of them are pretty young, I realize now, in the flickering yellow light at the end of the tunnel. One is probably not even twelve. One is right around my age.

The one who had my wrist seems to be the oldest—around Hunter's age, probably: almost sixty—and he's got a stubby and stinky cigar clenched between his big teeth, like Spider-Man's boss at the newspaper.

"What do you weirdoes want, anyway?" I say, wondering if I'm better off without Hunter's cash—or whether it would suffice to pay these thugs off.

"We don't want nothin'," says another of the guys from behind me. I can't see which of them is talking. But as he finishes talking, his words get higher and squished together, and then—BOOM—he sneezes. "Ain't that right, boys?"

The others mutter in agreement.

"My boys and I just want to be sure you're all right," says the first one—the old one with the stinky stogie. "Do we look like violent people to you?"

I turn, in the middle of this circle of strange men, and really check them all out.

They wear nice clothes—well past the expiration date. Their pants are stained and frayed. Their suit jackets are mismatched and ill-fitted. Their shirts are missing buttons and have collars the color of pee.

I find the oldest one's face again. "I don't know," I say. "I've never known a violent person."

"Never?" he says.

I nearly take it back. An image of my stepmother, with that insincere grin splashed across her face like a scar, appears in my mind. But what business is it of his?

So I say, "Never," and I cross my arms in front of myself.

He pulls the cigar from his mouth. "You're all right, then?" he asks.

"Peachy," I say.

"Then you live near here," he adds.

"Of course," I say.

And he shrugs. "If the kid don't want help," he says to his boys, "the kid don't get help. Let's head home."

The circle evaporates. Six men follow their elder from the tunnel, into the drizzle of the night. But one, as he steps out of the alcove, pauses and looks back at me. He's one of the younger ones, about my age.

"You sure?" he says as his friends or brothers or family walk off. "Because listen. I grew up on these streets, and I can spot an outsider, like finding a glittering coin in a heap of compost. You ain't a local."

I narrow my eyes at him, trying to look tough, like I belong, but in the back of my mind I know he can see my bathing suit through my sundress. And I know as well as he does that no one wanders the Bronx alone in a bathing suit under a sundress.

"You're also real pretty," he says. "I don't like the idea of you bein' on your own out here. Not at night, especially."

He's pretty too, somewhere under the grime of the streets and the yellowing of his clothes, so I pull my eyes away and look at my feet.

My shoes are wet. My feet are covered with the same grime he's wearing all over. But I say nothing.

"All right," he finally says—a vocal shrug. "I'll let you be." With that, he's jogging after the others.

When I'm alone in the flickering light at the mouth of the tunnel, unharmed and feeling like a fool, I call out. "Wait!" I say. I start running, taking my best guess where they headed. "I do need help. Please wait!"

I only run a quarter block before I find them—all seven, waiting in front of a 24-hour drugstore. The youngest one comes out of the pack. He's small for his age, looks like, and barely half my height, but he holds out a bright-yellow rain slicker, just bought. The tags are still on it.

"I bought it for you," he says.

I take it and pull it on and offer a very quiet

and embarrassed thank-you. The pretty one offers a soft grin, and the cigar smoker claps me on the shoulder and says, "Come on. We've got a safe place to wait out this rain and let you dry off."

The seven lead me down side streets, through alleys and holes in fences, and up five flights of crumbling steps in an old, red-brick building next to some overgrown train tracks.

"It's safe enough," says the pretty one. "I promise."

Ahead of us, the oldest pulls a key ring from his belt and unlocks no fewer than ten bolts. Then he swings open the heavy-looking metal door.

Inside is a big, empty room. When I say big, I mean almost the size of our palace on the park.

But this place doesn't have any of the comforts I'm used to at home. A few chairs sit randomly here and there, along with a pair of folding tables, set next to each other as if for family meals at Thanksgiving.

Along the length of the place, there are square, thick columns holding up the industrial ceiling. One wall is floor-to-ceiling windows, stained or painted green and black. In a handful of the windows, old-fashioned fans spin.

I follow the others inside and pull off my raincoat.

"Make yourself at home," says the oldest. "Then we'll do introductions and see what we can do for you."

He falls against a pile of pillows against the wall nearby. The others join him in a lazy slouch. I wonder if they're thinking I'll do the same as I pull a chair across the floor for myself. I place it near their lounging pile and sit.

"So," says the smoker as he pulls a half-smoked stogie from his pocket. "Who are you? What's your story?"

I wait a moment and cross my legs at the knees. "You first," I say, looking the oldest right in the eye.

He shrugs and smiles. "Fair enough," he says. "Seems to me you've had a pretty rough day. First of all, I'm Stogie."

Obviously.

He looks over the pile of boys and men, finally pointing at the youngest. "That's Sprite."

I smile at the boy, and he blushes and grins and looks away.

"He's bashful," said the oldest, "but he'll rob you blind."

Sprite takes a pebble from his coat pocket and wings at the oldest. The others laugh.

"Next is Snick." The pretty one, with beautiful, tired eyes and a mop of hair that's probably never been washed. "He made sure we helped you out tonight."

I nod at Snick, and he nods back. Stogie

runs through the rest of the group: Bright-Eyes, Stupid, Grumper, and Sneeze. I get a handshake, a dramatic bow, a grunt, and a booming achoo.

"And I'm Eira Blanc," I say.

The moment the words leave my lips, Stogie's eyebrows go up and Grumper sighs and grunts.

"What?" I say. "Do you know me?"

Stogie nods as Grumper gets up from his cushion, gives the brick wall a solid kick, and waddles off, deep into the empty warehouse.

"I don't get it," I say.

"Neither do I," says Snick, getting to his feet. "What's goin' on?"

"This," says Stogie, pointing at me with his namesake, "is the daughter—excuse me, stepdaughter—of none other than the Witch of the West Side."

A gasp. A hand on a mouth. A "whoa."

"The Witch of the—" I start to say. "Wait a minute. You've heard of my stepmom?"

They have, obviously, and they've got stories. From the youngest to the oldest, they start in with them, all talking at once, all on their feet or their knees, leaning toward me with excitement and wonder.

"Please," I say, my hands up, "not all at once." But over the noise of their own voices, no one's listening to me.

"Quiet!" comes a bellow from across the floor. It echoes through the cavernous space like a thunderclap.

And it works. All the voices stop, and we wait for Grumper to waddle back to our corner. When he does, he says in a voice so deep that it shakes my insides, "This is no time for stories. It's no time for shivering in fear, either. This girl is in trouble if she is who she says she is, and if we've helped her tonight, then we're in trouble too."

No one speaks. They look at me, and I look at my hands. Finally I mutter, "It's not as bad as that, is it?"

But it is—we all know it, and I know it especially, because if it were up to Stepmom, I'd be lying dead in an alley less than a mile from here, with the marks of Hunter's gloves around my throat.

"There's one story you need to hear," I say, and I tell them what's happened tonight so far.

~7~

"Let me get this straight," says Stupid. He's the tallest of the group, and the skinniest. He's got the same moppy hair as Snick, but none of his good looks otherwise. "You don't have the cash your driver gave you?"

"No," I say.

"You didn't accept it?" he says, leaning forward.

I shake my head.

"I do not understand people," Stupid says. "I never will."

"The money would have been helpful," Stogie says, "but it's not the point." He stands in front of my chair and puts a hand on my shoulder. "You can stay here, long as you need to—till it's safe for you to leave."

"Oh, no!" I say. "I don't need anything like that. I need to get back to the apartment. I need to make sure Hunter is okay. I need to make sure my father is okay!"

Stogie shakes his head, eyes closed and very calm. "You're crazy," he says. "If the Witch of the West Side wants you dead, she'll kill you. The minute you show up at that apartment—" And he drags his finger across his throat like a blade. "Dead."

I lean back and swallow hard.

"Listen, Eira," says Snick. I didn't notice him move, but he's on one knee next to my chair. He takes my hand. "The boys and Stogie—we know how to get around this town. All five boroughs. And we can keep an eye on your friends on the west side."

"But you're stayin' put," Stogie adds. He looks down at Snick and adds, "You and Bright-Eyes, set up someplace for our guest to sleep."

"Can do," says Snick. He motions toward Bright-Eyes, who grins—he always grins—and seems to float up from the cushions. The two walk clear across the space.

"But," I say as I get up from my chair, "I can't pay you."

"You'll help out around here," says Stogie. He takes my hand and leads me across the giant room. "You know the last time we had a home-cooked meal, or even swept the joint?"

"Most days we just have ketchup sandwiches on white bread," moans Grumper.

"Delicious!" says Stupid, and Grumper sighs his grumpiest sigh.

I don't mention I've never cooked anything more than toast. Before long, Snick and Bright-Eyes have set up a bed, barriers, and privacy screens.

"Thank you," I say.

Stogie leads into to my new bedroom, such as it is. He stays there with me till I sit down on the edge of the bed—it's really just a wood platform and an old straw mattress. It doesn't look comfortable. But I'm so tired, I know I'll be asleep quick. "We'll get you some clothes tomorrow," Stogie adds as he leaves. "Good night."

"Good night!" the others call out.

I pull off my sundress and curl up under a pair of musty and threadbare blankets. As I drift off to sleep, I can hear them talking—talking about me—on the other side of the barriers.

"The poor girl," says one—it's Stogie, I think.

"Is she going to be okay?" says Sprite in his pipsqueaky little voice.

"She's gotta be," says Snick, and a couple of them laugh.

"Ugh," says a rough and deep voice—it has to be Grumper. "He's in love with her."

"She's beautiful," says Snick. "Skin like snow. Lips like rubies. And hair like the black keys on a piano."

Ebony, he means. The last thing I have before I fall asleep is a memory of Mom saying just the same thing.

I'm the first awake. It's not even dawn; I can just make out a tiny piece of the Manhattan lights through a scratch in the paint on the window. The others are asleep in their corner of pillows, so I decide I better get started in my new position as homemaker.

I find an old t-shirt and a pair of shorts in a corner. They fit well enough. First things first: those windows. Without sunlight in here, we'll all go mad or get rickets or something. With a quick look around, I spot a flat blade. It's easy to find things when everything is out in the open and there's not much to begin with.

Trying not to imagine why the boys need a blade at all, I get to scraping.

* * *

I'm halfway done with my eighth window when Sprite comes up behind and tugs on my t-shirt.

"Whatcha doin'?" he says.

"Letting in some sunlight," I say with a smile as I stoop beside him. "It's so gloomy in here, don't you think?"

He doesn't seem to have an opinion on the matter.

Instead he says, "Stogie ain't gonna be happy about this."

Right on cue, Stogie sits up. I swear, a second ago he was fast asleep, snoring like a bear. But the instant Sprite said the old man's name, he sat up like a shot, jumped to his feet, and stormed across the wood-plank floor.

"Girly!" he snaps from half his mouth. How did he grab a cigar already? "What in the name of all that is good and holy are you doin'?!"

I've made him mad, it seems. "I thought I'd let some light in here," I say. My mouth twists and I add, "A lady's touch, right?"

He considers me, chewing on his unlit cigar, and calms down a bit. "The thing of it is," he says, dropping a beefy arm around my shoulders, "the boys and I, we like a little privacy."

"I see."

"Quite a lot of privacy, actually," he says.

I nod.

"In our particular line of work," he goes

on, walking me away from the window and gingerly prying the flat blade from my callused fingers, "a fair amount of secrecy is necessary."

"Line of work?" I say. The others are awake now, sitting up groggily on the pillows. Only Snick stays asleep, rolling onto his belly and snoring on.

Bright-Eyes hurries over, his eyes wide and tired, his mouth in a giant luminescent grin. "We're capital assessors and reinvestors."

"Well . . ." says Stogie.

"We're liberators," says Sneeze. He sniffles and coughs. "Of funds and financials."

"I don't know . . ." says Stogie.

"We're Robin Hood!" Sprite says, and Stogie chuckles.

Snick sits up and leans back on his arms. "We're thieves," he says. "We're good-for-nothing, scum-of-the-earth crooks, liars, robbers, and cheats."

Stogie shrugs. "Not to put too fine a point on it," he says.

"Oh," I say. I look at my feet. There they are, dirty as they were last night, and this morning my fingers—covered in dry flecks of paint, red with calluses and little nicks and cuts—make a matching set.

"You're disappointed," says Stogie, and I nearly protest, but he cuts me off. "But we never hurt no one."

Sprite shakes his head vigorously.

"Not a fly," says Bright-Eyes through his smile.

Snick walks up and takes my hand from Stogie. "But we work hard at what we do," he says, "and we do it well. So we know this city and its people."

"Especially the nasty ones," says Grumper from end of the room, where he's examining my handiwork on the windows. "We'll need thick curtains. Pronto."

"Which is why," Snick goes on, holding my eyes in his, "you'll stay here, while we do our work and see what the witch is up to this morning." He lets go of my hands and grabs his backpack on his way to the door.

Stogie claps me on the back as the rest of the crew gets the gear together. "The old dame might not even know you're still alive," he says with a wink.

"But it's a long shot," adds Grumper. He shoulders a pack that looks heavy and heads for the door.

I bend over so Sprite can give me a hug around the neck. "Don't open the door for anyone," he whispers at my ear. "Same rule as when I was little."

"You're not little anymore?" I ask him, and he shakes his head, his eyes squinty and twisted like I'd asked the dumbest question ever.

Then they're gone, so I find a broom. It looks like it's probably been here longer than the seven thieves, like maybe back in the day, this building was actually a house for storing wares.

I get to work. Just call me Cinderella.

9

I'm not very good at this. That's the first problem. I've never actually held a broom before, and maybe it's because this one is shockingly old, but the straw bundled at the end—which is supposed to be helping me gather dust and detritus into nice tidy piles—is itself falling out of the broom and becoming more mess to clean up.

The second problem is the seven thieves.

There doesn't seem to be any rhyme or reason
to how they live, and when I sweep up a pile
of twigs, rubber bands, three little stones,
and a sock, I don't know if I've made a pile
of garbage—or of some of their most prized
possessions.

After a solid three hours of sweeping,
though, I've created five piles, one of which—I
think—must be trash. That's when someone
bellows outside.

"Yoo-hoo!"

From the newly cleaned windows I can see
her down there, wrapped in a gray shawl, with
a black and white scarf tied around her white
hair.

"Please, pretty child," she calls up at me,
rubbing her hands together as if she's freezing
in the cold—though it's summer. She's covered
in rags, but she seems really kind. The sort of
old lady that you'd expect to see in some old
movie, but not in real life.

She's waving at me. "Please," she says. "I'm very hungry."

"I'm sorry," I call down. "I have nothing to give you!" It's probably true, unless there's a kitchen hidden around here someplace.

"Then at least let me come in to warm up," she says.

Is she kidding? But she's on the verge of tears, judging from the strain in her voice. What choice do I have?

"Come up," I shout down. "I'll let you in."

I hurry across the floor and open all ten bolts, then pull open the door. It is heavy, and when it's open all the way, I gasp.

"Good morning," says the woman.

"H-how did you get up here so fast?" I ask. "It's five flights."

"Was it?" she says, hobbling past me into the apartment. "I hardly noticed."

She pulls off her headscarf and shoves it

into her shawl someplace. "Now," she says, holding my arm for support, and at the same time leading me deeper into the big empty room. "Let's see what these lads have in the kitchen."

"Wait, what?" I say, trying to stop her. But she's strong—so much stronger than she looks. "Do you know these guys?"

She giggles—kind of. It sounds like a dry leaf bouncing along a sidewalk, plus the bells of an old-fashioned ice cream cart—and just as chilly. "My beautiful child," she croaks, "everyone knows 'these guys.'"

She takes me across the huge space, right up to the far wall, and stops.

"Um," I say. "The end. Can't walk any further."

But she lets go of my arm, puts a hand on the wall, and presto! A door appears.

She pushes it open, and there it is: the kitchen.

"Whoa," I say as she totters inside.

"Come, come," she says. "Don't stand there ogling. Time to start cooking lunch."

~10~

There's a tall stool in this magical kitchen—
as tall as the old lady herself—but she
manages to climb it and perch there. From its
top, she directs me around the kitchen. I go
from the magical fridge to the magical stove,
and from the magical cutting board to the
magical sink. Soon I've chopped onions and
carrots and potatoes and rutabagas and celery
root and so many herbs that I lose count.

"All of it, into the pot," she instructs, always smiling, always pleasant, and I obey.

Before long, the biggest shining pot in the kitchen is full almost to the rim, bubbling and steaming, filling the cavernous apartment with the most amazing smells.

"There is only one more ingredient," she says. She's got a bag on her lap. I didn't notice it when she came in, but it's some kind of lumpy old lady's purse. She's digging through it. "Ah! Here it is."

She pulls out a tiny yellow envelope and holds it out to me.

"What is it?" I ask, and I open the little top and bring it to my nose. It smells heavenly.

"Don't inhale too much, beautiful," she says. "On its own, it's far too strong."

It is strong, but so delicious smelling. I find it difficult to pull the envelope from my face. "Dump it in?" I ask.

She nods, so I do. The soup seems to bubble a little more as the powder sinks in, as if it, too, is relishing the flavor of the spice.

"Now, we wait," she says, and she drops from the stool and takes my arm. "Let's get some cleaning done around here, yes?"

This old woman is wonderful. She's fixed the broom and produced another from a hidden closet. She's taught me to mop, and she's helped me scrape the windows.

I can't believe the thieves have a friend like this woman. Why is their place so messy all the time?

"I'll have to ask them about it," I mumble aloud.

"Ask them what, my pretty dear?" asks the woman.

"Oh, I was just wondering," I say. "Why do the seven thieves live like slobs when they have a friend like you, perfectly willing to help out around here?"

She clucks her tongue—it sounds oddly familiar. "Oh, you doll," she says. "Men like that don't want an old hag like me hanging about. They prefer a pretty young thing."

Like me.

I know she means it as a compliment, but it reminds me of the back-handed comments Queen Stepmom would offer, when she caught me checking my hair in the mirror by the front door as I put on my coat before school, or while I lay out on the deck under the summer sun, trying to darken my snow-white skin—and failing to bronze at all.

Giselle says Stepmom is jealous. She always says Stepmom is jealous.

But my stepmother is a grown woman. She's married and she has riches unimaginable to 99 percent of the world.

Why would she be jealous of a sixteen-year-old girl? It's insane.

Then again, she did try to kill me, like, yesterday.

I stare at my hand as I work on a stubborn bit of scuff. My hand is ragged and red, and the rag it's pushing across the floor is dirty. "Oh," I say, a bit meek—meeker than I like, to be honest.

I snap out of it when the old lady claps, like a mosquito came too close: it's sudden and sharp. But it wasn't bug; it was a notion.

"Do you smell it?" she says, leaning her mop against the nearest steel column.

I sniff the air, and then shrug. "The chili, my dear," she says, lifting me by the armpit. She's stronger than she looks. "It's ready."

I sniff the air again, and yes—there it is!

It's delightful, too. Rich and spicy and intoxicating. I'm almost light-headed as she pulls me toward the kitchen—the kitchen revealed behind the magical door.

The magical door, I think somewhere in my muddled mind. *The magical kitchen. The magical broom closet, too.*

"Come, come," she says, because I'm stumbling over my own feet. I'm drowsy. I'm floating. The smell of the chili and the sound of her voice make me dizzy.

"I'm coming," I say. "It smells . . . it smells very good."

"Yes," she says. The *s* at the end of the word is like a leaking tire or a stream of sand. It makes me sleepy.

"Oh, I'm so tired," I say.

"You've been working hard, dear," she says. We've reached the kitchen now and she deposits me on a chair. "You're just hungry. I'll get you a bowl."

The bowl is in front of me already, and the spoon is in my hand.

"It's not too hot," she says, right at my ear, and it tickles a little when she whispers, "Taste it."

It's delicious. It's spicy and sweet and rich and fresh. It's like every flavor of the city in one spoonful—all its people and all its history and all its warm summer nights and frigid winter mornings. The bowl is empty now.

"It's wonderful," I tell her. "I'd like some more."

"When you wake, beautiful child," she says, because, of course, I'm in bed now, and the kind old lady pulls the covers up to my chin. "When you wake, you will have more."

"Yes," I say, a little smile forming on my face. I close my eyes.

The old lady runs her hand gently over my head, pushing my hair back from my forehead. It's nice.

"You're such a pretty girl," she says, and her voice is smoother now—still tiring, still gentle, but without the roughness of a long life. And it's familiar.

"Your lips," she says, "are so red, the color of blood. And your hair"—her hand pauses atop my head—"as black as ebony."

I want to open my eyes. I cannot.

"But your skin," she says, and she runs the backs of her fingers over my cheek, "is the most lovely of all."

I know her voice now. This is no old woman. I want to grab her wrist and snap it, but my hands won't move.

"So white and soft and clear," she says, "like snow."

Why can't I open my eyes?

"Beautiful Eira," she says in her true voice—my stepmother's voice. "Your mother must have been very beautiful indeed."

She stands; I feel her weight leave the bed beside me. "Sleep well, princess," she says. "Sleep forever."

~12~

They're back. The seven of them stand around my bed. Still, I can't move. I can't open my eyes.

It's lucky I can breathe, I suppose.

I wonder if Bright-Eyes is grinning. Sprite is crying, sounds like.

"It was the witch," says Grumper. "She was here. I can still smell her in this place. It's like sulfur."

"And . . ." says Sneeze, and his voice goes high and nasal, "cayenne pepper. Achoo!"

"I knew the girl would be trouble," Grumper grumbles.

"Enough of that," says Stogie. "No point standin' around goin' over what the problem is. We all know what the problem is. The point now is to solve it."

"Should we take her to the hospital?" one of them asks.

Someone else laughs. "No. How would we explain her being here? We have to figure out something else."

"I'll kill her," says a voice, thick and quiet. "That'll end any curse: kill the witch."

"Don't be a fool, Snick," says Stogie. "Even if you could get close enough to her, she'd snap you in two like a dry old twig. You'll stay here with Sprite, keep an eye on Eira. Clear?"

"Fine," says Snick, but I can tell that he's

sure not happy about it. "What's your plan, then?"

Stogie is chomping on his cigar. It's lit today, and the smell—though strong and awful—is comforting somehow. I can't see them. I can't reach out for Snick's hand. But I can smell Stogie's cigar, and that's something.

"We'll go into Manhattan," Stogie says through his teeth. "Tonight. Right now. And we'll get inside her house."

No! I want to shout. *You must not do that. She'll kill you all!*

But I can't. With all my strength, I will my arms to move to grab Stogie. I urge my mouth to open, my eyes to widen. But I have no strength, and I have no will, and I lie there like a useless lump.

"She'll kill you," says Snick. He sits on the edge of the bed—or I think it's him. It's hard to say for sure.

"We won't confront her," says Stogie, and

he sits beside Snick. Maybe he puts that meaty arm around his shoulder. I wonder if they're father and son. They don't look it—at least, not genetically. "We'll snoop around, like we do. We'll take what we can—anything relevant."

Grumper laughs. "We won't find a flashing sign that says 'Spell books in here,'" he says.

Stogie chuckles. "We'll find something," he says, and I can hear the smile in his voice. I can also hear it fade when he adds, "We have to."

The bed shifts as Stogie gets up. Their footsteps ring and stomp and drag across the huge floor. The door opens and closes, the slam ringing through the giant apartment. And the five are gone, and Sprite sniffles at my bedside.

"We won't let you go, Eira," whispers Snick. He puts a hand on mine. "I promise."

~13~

Snick won't sit down. He just walks back and forth and around my bed, now and then kneeling briefly to press his forehead against the back of my hand.

I'm not dead, I want to scream at him. I can't, of course. I can't do anything at all.

Now and then, I drift off to sleep—somehow. Sleep is better than wakefulness today, because when I sleep, I can see and I can move. I can jump up from the bed and throw my arms around Snick.

I don't know why, but since I've been lying here I've wanted nothing more than a kiss—a kiss from Snick.

Right on the mouth.

* * *

Sprite's asleep now. I can hear his snoring from the corner.

If I could move, I'd have to twist my neck halfway around to see him, but I can picture him, with his knees pulled up and his head down on his knees, his arms wrapped around, so he's a little snoring ball.

Snick is worn out too. He's pulled a second chair right up to my bed, and he's holding my hand.

I can feel the warmth and the pressure, but

I can't wrap my fingers around his. I can't twist our fingers together.

"Oh, Eira. I don't know if you can hear me, sweetheart," he says, his voice rough and tired. "But we're going to help you. I promise. My brothers will be back soon, and they'll know how to fix this."

I have no idea how long they've been gone. Without movement, without sight, with only dreams and a thief boy's hand to keep me company, time hardly exists. It could have been an hour; it's probably been a day and a night.

"You're so beautiful," he says, and his voice is now gentle and even joyful.

"I know, I know," he says, as if I've responded—did my lips move? I wanted to smile. "I hardly know you. Heck, I don't actually know you at all." He's up and pacing again. My hand feels cold and heavy.

"It's probably just magic," he says, and I'm afraid his heavy steps across the cement floor will wake Sprite, and then Snick won't keep talking to me.

Sprite only snores on, though, even as Snick's voice gets nasty and he says, "You probably picked it up, hanging around in that witch's palace."

What? I think. *How dare he?*

"How else could you explain it?" he says, and he drops back into the chair. "Why else would I fall in love with some rich girl from the west side? Why else would I even care?" His voice is soft again.

Love?

He's right; it must be magic.

"Every time I take your hand," he says, "I expect it to be cold."

The thought chills me, but his hands are warm, and soon I'm warmed right through.

"Your stepmother is very smart," he says, whispering, "and very powerful. But she's evil.

Right down to the center of her heart, she's evil. We might just be some lousy pack of common thieves, but we have good hearts, you know?"

He stands, still holding my hand. "Oh, I don't even know what I'm saying," he says. "You probably can't hear me anyway."

Oh, but I can!

"If you can hear me . . ." he says. Then his voice is right next to my ear. I can feel the warmth of his breath on my neck. "Forgive me for this."

His lips press against mine gently, and it's like I'm coming up from the bottom of a crystal-clear lake.

My body fills up with breath and life. The tingle of the kiss spreads across my face and down my neck and all over my body.

My eyes open—I can open my eyes! I can lift my arms, and I can wrap them around Snick's body.

"Whoa!" he says, and he jumps up from the bed.

I laugh and smile up at him. "Hello."

~14~

We're sitting there on the bed, his hand in mine, and his cheeks as red as delicious apples when the rest of the guys slam through the door.

They're all shouting:

"We're back!" they bellow.

"We know!" they holler.

"It is magic!" they roar.

"We know what to do!" they scream.

Their footsteps thunder along the cement floor of the apartment.

Stogie's voice rises above the rest like a steamship foghorn. "A kiss!" he shouts. "She must be kissed by the one she loves—"

And he stops short, and they screech to a halt as they come around the side of the blind and into my funny little bedroom.

"Ah," says Stogie, shuffling like the others, looking at his feet.

He pulls a cigar from his vest pocket. The cigar is half smoked and tattered at its tip. He sticks it between his teeth, while Snick's face gets somehow redder.

"Kissed her, then?" says Grumper as he lifts his chin and looks down his nose at me and Snick.

It breaks the ice, and the rest of them can laugh. I drop my head onto Snick's shoulder and giggle along with them.

"That's that dealt with," Grumper says. "But there's still a witch to deal with."

"Do we have to?" I say, looking from eager thief to eager thief. "I'm okay now. She won't come after me again."

Stogie sits on my other side on the bed as Grumper gives Sprite a hard shove to wake him up.

"The witch tried to poison you, Eira," Stogie says. "We'll not let her get away with that, will we?"

I check Snick. He shakes his head at me and squeezes my hand a little tighter.

"You can say no," he whispers, though in the dead-quiet warehouse, he might as well have shouted.

"Stogie's right," I say, getting to my feet. "And I know who might help us."

~15~

I've been gone less than three days, but my apartment building on the west side feels like a foreign country to me now.

At the entrance to the underground parking garage is a woman walking her three purebred Pomeranians. She's head-to-toe in boutique fashions, with one leash in one hand and two in the other, and chatting away on her hands-free cell phone, laughing and cackling.

I slip in through the pedestrian entrance—no key required; it's a keypad entry. Just then, a classic Jaguar coupe zips up the ramp. The engine sings and roars like a real Jaguar as it squeals around the tight little bends of the garage and out into the nighttime Manhattan streets.

There's no echo tonight as I cross the huge cement garage. My feet are bare and silent, free of the clip-clopping heels I'd usually have on. Hunter doesn't know I'm there until I'm right behind him.

"Eira!" he shouts, rather by accident, I think. When I laugh at his reaction, he shushes me and pulls me out of the light and into a dark corner behind the family limo. "What are you doing here?"

"I live here," I say, mostly as a joke. But it's true—I think.

He grabs my wrist—a little too hard—and growls at me. "I told you never to come back here," he says. "She'll tear my head off if she finds out I've been talking to you."

I tug my hand away and he lets me go. His shoulders droop as he goes on. "She has a way of finding things out."

"If that's so," I say, "then she must know that you let me go in that alley instead of wringing my neck."

His eyes go wide and then close in despair. Through a frown, he says, "She was looking at me in an especially strange way over her soup spoon as she ate this evening."

"Then she'll have your head no matter what," I say. "Unless you help me stop her."

He looks at me sideways, his eyes narrowed. "What exactly did you have in mind, princess?"

"First tell me," I say. "Will you help?"

I've never seen Hunter look so horrible and gray. His back slumps even farther, and his eyes close, as if he's expecting the blade of a guillotine.

"Remember how it used to be?" I prod. "Before the witch lived with us. You were so committed to my parents—to my real mother."

He opens his eyes and they soften. "You look more like her every day." He even smiles— just the tiniest bit—and I know he's with us.

"Okay," I call into the darkness of the garage. "You can come out!"

The seven thieves emerge from the darkness—Sprite from beneath a nearby SUV, Stogie from behind a hefty column—and stand in their motley circle around us. I find Snick's hand and pull him into the circle.

"This is Snick," I tell Hunter. "He's in love with me."

"Aw, Eira," Snick says, and his face goes red. I'm finding it fun to make him blush already.

"I don't blame him," says Hunter, his eyes

still on me. "Ach," he goes on, slapping himself on the forehead, "how could I have been so weak? How could I have let that witch control me for so long?"

"It's not your fault," Stogie says as he chomps his cigar. "She's a powerful witch. It'd take a very strong man to stand up to her."

Hunter throws back his shoulders—it's like throwing off a heavy, musty blanket he's had over his head since Mom died—and looks me right in the eyes. "Then that's what I'll have to be."

~16~

The thieves and I crouch between cars, huddled together like wolf pups during a storm, anxious for their first hunt.

From where I'm kneeling—with Stogie on one side and Snick on the other, his hand on my shoulder, heavy and present—I can see Hunter lean across the roof of the limo.

He's rubbing a stubborn spot with a soft cloth. He knows the smallest things send Her Highness into a fit of rage.

And finally she appears. One of the building's doormen appears first, of course. It's Antoine, and he's wearing the garage doorman jacket, which is black with red stripes instead of red with gold. It's all pomp and circumstance around here.

Antoine steps through the door and holds it open, standing far back with his eyes on his feet. That's his most professional pose. If it were me coming through the door—and if I didn't quickly say "Don't get up!" as I hurried past—he'd be smiling. We might even high five.

Then Her Majesty steps through. She wears her finest coat—I wonder where she thinks she's going. It's down to her ankles and billows out in a ring of white fur trim, which runs all the way up the coat and around the collar. I've seen it before; she can pull up a hood of the same fine red fabric and white fur trim. You might think a coat like that would remind you of Santa Claus, but you'd be wrong. There is nothing joyful about it.

"Already nearly nine," she says as she strides up to the limo. "You'll have to make up the time on the road."

"Yes, ma'am," says Hunter. He pulls open the passenger door and, as she takes his hand and climbs in, catches my eye—only for an instant. I smile and flash a thumbs-up. Hunter closes the witch's door and gets into the driver's seat. They're off.

As the car slides up the ramp at Hunter's predictably safe pace, Stogie gets to his feet and groans. With his hands on his lower back, he stretches and says, "We'd better hurry. I don't think your valet, good a man as he is, stands a chance without a little support from us."

I grab Snick's hand as I stand up. "Then let's run."

～17～

The police station isn't far, and thanks to typical Manhattan cross-town traffic, Hunter and Stepmom have only been there a few minutes when the thieves and I barrel into the waiting area.

Even before the arrival of seven thieves and a sixteen-year-old girl in a tattered sundress and with dirty bare feet, the police station's lobby area is a madhouse.

Four uniformed cops—New York's finest—
stand around, all staring. They've taken off
their caps in respect, and they look at Stepmom
and smile and babble. A couple of detectives,
in their dress shirts with wet armpits and
loosened ties, lean on the high counter and
flutter their eyes. Hunter, the poor good-
hearted man, has removed his cap as well. He
wrings it in his hands like a wet rag and nods
and bows in apology.

And in the middle of it all? Of course,
it's Stepmom. Her glorious red coat is open,
revealing a shimmering white cocktail dress
subtly speckled with diamond dust. Her arms
are up and open, and her soul seems to absorb
the adoration of the men who surround her.

That is a lie, though. Really the men absorb
her magic—it comes from her like a foul
poison scented with perfume.

"Stop this!" I shout at once. I shove through
two cops and a pair of cuffed criminals. They

don't notice me, but I don't mind. I stand face-to-face with Stepmom—or as near as I can. In her mile-high heels, and with my bare feet, the top of my head hardly reaches her chin.

"Stop what, my dearest daughter?" she says, her mouth wide and smiling. "I've had the strangest evening."

Hunter sees me and it's like a light flicks on in his brain. He tugs at his hat, struggles to make it smooth, and slaps it onto his head. "I've been trying, Eira," he says. "I really have, I swear."

Stogie is beside him now and holding his arm. "You've done fine, man," he says. Then he faces the witch. "It's over, my lady," he says. "If you please, lower your arms and remove your spell from these good people."

"Why is he being so polite?" I whisper to Snick.

"You should always be polite to witches," he replies. "Everyone knows that."

I shrug, since I didn't know that, but these thieves seem to know the city and its secrets way better than I do.

Polite or not, the witch laughs at Stogie. "Take that cigar out of your mouth, you filthy mongrel," she says. I guess the politeness rule doesn't work both ways.

Stogie nods pleasantly and removes the cigar from his teeth. "As you wish," he says. I wonder for a moment if he, too, is falling under the spell. "But if you please, end this spell and surrender for your crime."

Stepmom leans over and laughs in his face—right in his face! With her mouth only inches from his nose. Still, he smiles and nods.

"Not you too," says one of the detectives behind the counter. He wears a thick and dark mustache that nearly hides the magical-lovesick smile on his lips. "Her driver made the most absurd accusations. He claimed this lovely woman was a murderer."

"She is!" I scream over the laughter of adoring policemen. "She poisoned me!" The room fills with laughter.

Hunter catches my eye, and his are wet.

"Please, listen," I call over the roar of laughter. Though my thieves are safe from the witch's spell of adoration, the policemen and other criminals in the lobby are nearly doubled over. They think it's the funniest thing ever, that their new object of love and desire could ever harm another.

"Aren't there any female police officers in this precinct?" Snick says to me.

Hunter is still watching me. His eyes are still wet, but he throws back his shoulders. He seems to grow half a foot—as tall as the witch now, although he seemed bent and beaten on seconds ago.

He sees my mother in my face, and it gives him strength. I push through the crowd and take his hand. "Help me."

He nods and he calls out. "It's all true." The laughter surges, but he goes on. "This woman poisoned her own stepdaughter."

I nod at him, urge him on, despite the thundering jeers of the policemen. Around us, the thieves clamp their hands over mouths, struggling to stifle the laughter.

"Her stepdaughter?" one of the detectives says through gasps for air and huge guffaws. "Isn't that her stepdaughter, right next to you?"

He pats a handcuffed thug on the shoulder. "She look poisoned to you?" he says. For a split second, the laughter stops. Then it erupts with more hysterical violence.

Hunter—his eyes still on mine, and still red and filling with tears—shakes his head and slumps his shoulders. He stares at his feet. He can't go on, and I realize now why.

I take my stepmother by the wrists and pull her arms down to her sides. The men stop their laughter. A couple even growl a little, their stares on me now, like attack dogs snarling at a burglar.

"She tried to kill me," I say, my gaze fixed on the witch. She looks right back, and though her stare is usually enough to subdue me— enough even to burn an ant on the sidewalk, like a ray of sunshine through a magnifying glass—tonight, it only gives me strength. "She murdered my mother."

There are gasps. Snick puts a hand on my arm. Stogie replaces his cigar and chews it and closes his eyes like a mourner.

"It's true, isn't it, Hunter?" I say. He nods, like I knew he would. He looks beaten and sad, but I don't blame him. I'm not even sure he believed it himself, although deep down, I think he and I always knew the truth. Her spell kept us from seeing it.

"You've done it, Eira," says Hunter. "Her magic is fading."

He's right. Around us, police officers rub

their eyes and stretch and yawn, like they've just woken up. The witch's smile is drooping and weak.

We've beaten her, I think. It took seven thieves—seven wonderful boys and men I hardly know—and a valet whose love for me and my mom was not enough on its own. It also took my own love for my mom and the tears that now run down my cheeks.

~18~

I'm back in the office. This time, though, I'm not waiting for my stepmother. I'm practically holding my breath, watching my father pace across the huge red rug that sits in the center of the room.

And I'm watching from her side of the big desk, too, in her big chair.

I'm also secretly hoping that—once my dad has had some time to come to grips with what's happened—he'll let me redecorate in here and make it just like it was before the witch came along.

"I can hardly believe what you've told me," he says. He looks from me to Hunter, seated in the guest chair.

Then Dad lets his eyes slowly pass over the seven thieves, lined up against the long bookcase, all of them with their hats and caps off and grinning as pleasantly and honestly as they know how. Stogie doesn't even have his cigar.

"But I know I must," Dad says with a tired sigh. He leans on the desk beside me and pushes my hair back from my forehead. "I was in my hotel room in Tokyo, and I just . . . felt it." He stares out the window behind me at the setting sun. "It was as if someone pulled a blindfold off me, or flicked on the light . . ."

"Or pulled a blanket off your head," says Hunter.

"Or showed you the truth in your heart," I say, and I take my father's hand.

"Yes," he says. "All those things."

I stand and put my arms around him. "She's gone now," I say. "The witch is gone, and we can start to make things right."

We hold each other till someone coughs. I open my eyes and see Stogie, a shy smile on his face.

"Forgive me," he says. "We've taken up too much of your time, and we'll leave now and let you handle your family business in private."

"Ah," Dad says. He sits me back down and in two long strides stands in front of Stogie. "A band of thieves," he says. "How very . . . Robin Hoodish."

Sprite says, "Ha!" and points. "See? See?" he says.

Stogie chuckles and shushes the boy. "We're not nearly as noble as we seem," he says.

"Think you've got a huge bag of money coming to you?" Dad says as he crosses his arms across his huge chest. "A handsome reward?"

Stogie reaches into his coat pocket for a cigar stub. "It's nothing like that," he says. He looks down the line of thieves at Snick and winks. Dad sees it and steps down the line to look down his nose at Snick.

"Oh, no," I mutter. "Dad, please, let him be."

"So?" Dad says in his deepest, most intimidating voice. He may not have the witch's magic—I refuse to call her Stepmother any longer—but he can be just as persuasive. "What is it you want? A reward? Maybe a job—a good position with my firm?"

"No—no sir," Snick says. He squeezes his hat in his hands and his face reddens. It's tough not to jump from my seat and take his hand to pull him away from Dad.

But I've forgotten. He's so kind and shy, but he's also a boy who grew up in the Bronx, living day to day with a band of thieves. Of course he can handle one man—even a man like Dad.

"What I'd really like," Snick says, "is your permission to date Eira."

Dad's eyes go wide and he gasps and stutters a moment, and now he's blushing. Everyone in the room—except Snick and my dad, of course—busts up laughing at the sight of Dad speechless and red-faced. Even Dad has to smile—and that's not something he's fond of doing.

He looks over his shoulder at me. "What about it, princess?" he says. "Do you want to date a thief from the Bronx?"

"More than anything," I say. I feel my face get hot as I smile back at him and then at Snick.

"All right, then," says Dad, looking Snick right in the face and putting out his hand to

shake. Snick takes it—though it's bigger than his by two. "And maybe we'll see about getting you that job, too. I can't have my daughter dating a criminal."

Snick says, "Thanks!"

Dad looks over the other thief faces. "And that goes for the rest of you, too," he says. "If you'll have the jobs."

The thieves say their thank-yous, and Dad takes them around to meet the rest of the staff. Snick hangs back. "I can hardly believe my luck," he says as he moves toward me.

I swivel the big desk chair to face the window. The sun is nearly down now, and I can see Snick's reflection in the plate glass.

He comes up behind my chair and puts his hands on my shoulders and leans down. I close my eyes and feel him press his lips against the top of my head. I feel his breath as he whispers, "The fairest girl in the city."

Snow White
and the
Seven Dwarves

• ★ • ★ •

Snow White is a German fairy tale first published by the Brothers Grimm in their 1812 collection. But the tale itself is probably much older. In fact, there is an Albanian version of the tale that may date from as long ago as the Middle Ages.

In the original story, Snow White's father, the King, has married a cruel woman who is incredibly vain. Each day, Snow White's stepmother looks into her magic mirror and asks whether she's the most beautiful person in the land. The mirror always says that she is—until one day it tells her that Snow White has become much more beautiful.

This angers the queen, and she instructs a huntsman to take Snow White into the woods and kill her.

But the huntsman can't do it. He brings Snow White to the woods and leaves her there. While wandering, Snow White finds a tiny cottage that's home to seven dwarves. But her evil stepmother quickly finds out that she's there. The queen dresses up as an old woman and goes to the cottage, where she sells Snow White a poisoned apple.

The apple sends Snow White into a magic sleep. The dwarves can't figure out how to wake her. But a prince passes through the forest, kisses Snow White, and heals her.

The Queen dies, but the prince and Snow White marry and live happily ever after.

Tell your own twicetold tale!

• ★ • ★ •

Choose one from each group, and write a story that combines all of the elements you've chosen.

A little girl who is lost

A boy who can't stop dreaming about Paris

A princess who loses her voice

A young man who loves horses

A suburban house

A fire station

A crumbling castle

A tent

A one-eyed cat

A donkey

A songbird

A whale

A leather shoe

A lace glove

A gold chain

A glass apple

China

Buenos Aires

A German forest

A tiny town

A kind queen

A gnome

A tired peddler

A baby with green eyes

TWICE TOLD TALES

Cassie and the Woolf

by Olivia Snowe

TWICE TOLD TALES

The Sealed-Up House

by Olivia Snowe

TWICE TOLD TALES

A Home in the Sky

by Olivia Snowe

about the author

Olivia Snowe lives between the falls, the forest, and the creek in Minneapolis, Minnesota.

about the illustrator

Michelle Lamoreaux was born and raised in Utah. She studied at Southern Utah University and graduated with a BFA in illustration. She likes working with both digital and traditional media. She currently lives and works in Cedar City, Utah.